My First
ACTION
RHYMES

pictures by Lynne Cravath

SCHOLASTIC INC.

New York Toronto London Auckland Sydney
Mexico City New Delhi Hong Kong Buenos Aires

My First
ACTION RHYMES

For Macklin—let's play!
—L. C.

The original publisher would like to acknowledge Emilie Poulsson for "Here Is The Beehive"

ISBN 0-439-31411-9

Compilation copyright © 2000 by HarperCollins Publishers.
Illustrations copyright © 2000 by Lynne W. Cravath.
All rights reserved.
Published by Scholastic Inc., 555 Broadway, New York, NY 10012,
by arrangement with HarperCollins Children's Books,
a division of HarperCollins Publishers.
SCHOLASTIC and associated logos are trademarks and/or
registered trademarks of Scholastic Inc.

12   8 9 10 11 12/0

Printed in the U.S.A.   23

First Scholastic printing, October 2001

Designed by Tom Starace

If You're Happy and You Know It

If you're happy and you know it,
Clap your hands.

> *(Clap your hands twice.)*

If you're happy and you know it,
Clap your hands.

> *(Clap your hands twice.)*

If you're happy and you know it,
And you really want to show it,
If you're happy and you know it,
Clap your hands.

> *(Clap your hands twice.)*

Continue with:

If you're mad and you know it, stamp your feet. . . .
If you're excited and you know it, wave your arms. . . .
If you're sad and you know it, rub your eyes. . . .
If you're silly and you know it, shake your head. . . .

Head, Shoulders, Knees and Toes

Head, shoulders, knees and toes, knees and toes.
Head, shoulders, knees and toes, knees and toes,
And eyes and ears and mouth and nose.
Head, shoulders, knees and toes, knees and toes!

(Touch each body part as it is named.)

The Beehive

Here is the beehive.
(Make a fist.)
Where are the bees?
Hidden away where nobody sees.
(Point to fist.)
Here they come creeping out of their hive—
One, two, three, four, five!
*(Slowly lift thumb and fingers
one at a time.)*
They're alive!
Bzzzz.
(Wiggle fingers.)

I'm a Little Teapot

I'm a little teapot,
Short and stout.
Here is my handle.
(Put one hand on hip.)
Here is my spout.
(Bend other arm out to the side like a spout.)
When I get all steamed up,
(Jump up.)
Hear me shout,
"Tip me over and pour me out!"
(Tip body sideways.)

Five Fat Peas

Five fat peas in a peapod pressed.
>   *(Clasp both hands together in a fist.)*

One grew, two grew,
>   *(Extend thumbs together and then extend*
>   *index fingers together.)*

And so did all the rest.
>   *(Continue extending fingers.)*

They grew, and they grew, and they never stopped.
>   *(Move hands apart slowly.)*

They grew so fat that the peapod POPPED!
>   *(Clap hands together on the word "popped.")*

The Hammer Song

Jenny* pounds with one hammer,
> *(Move one hand up and down repeatedly like a hammer.)*

One hammer, one hammer.

Jenny pounds with one hammer.

Then she pounds with two.

> *Continue with:*
> Jenny pounds with two hammers. . . .
> > *(Move two hands up and down.)*
>
> Jenny pounds with three hammers. . . .
> > *(Stamp one foot up and down while moving both hands.)*
>
> Jenny pounds with four hammers. . . .
> > *(Jump up and down while moving both hands.)*

Jenny pounds with five hammers,
> *(Nod head up and down while continuing*
> *all other motions.)*

Five hammers, five hammers.

Jenny pounds with five hammers,

Then she goes to sleep!
> *(Rest head on folded hands.)*

*(*Substitute your child's name.)*

The Elephant

An elephant goes like this and that.

 (Clasp hands together with arms extended in
 front of you and sway arms back and forth.)

He's oh, so big,

 (Stretch arms up high.)

And he's oh, so fat.

 (Put arms out to the side.)

He has no fingers,

And he has no toes,

 (Put two fists in front of you.)

But goodness gracious,

What a nose!

 (Extend clasped hands in front of face like a nose.)

Balloons

This is the way we blow our balloon.
Blow! Blow! Blow!
*(Place hands on cheeks and
gradually puff cheeks out.)*
This is the way we break our balloon.
Oh, oh, no!
("Pop" cheeks to blow out air.)

Five Little Ducks

Five little ducks
That I once knew.
(Hold up five fingers.)
Fat ducks, skinny ducks,
Fair ducks, too.
(Wiggle fingers.)

But the one little duck
With a feather on his back,
(Hold up pointer finger.)
He led the others with
A quack, quack, quack.
*(Open and close fingers against
thumb to imitate a duck's bill.)*

Down to the river
They would go,
Wibble-wobble, wibble-wobble,
To and fro.
*(With palms together, move hands
back and forth.)*

But the one little duck
With a feather on his back,
(Hold up pointer finger.)
He led the others with
A quack, quack, quack!
Quack, quack, quack.
Quack, quack, quack.
He led the others with
A quack, quack, quack!
*(Open and close fingers against
thumb to imitate a duck's bill.)*

Where Is Thumbkin?

Where is Thumbkin?
Where is Thumbkin?
>   *(Begin with two fists behind back.)*

Here I am!
>   *(Bring out one fist with thumb raised.)*

Here I am!
>   *(Bring out other fist with thumb raised.)*

How are you today, sir?
>   *(Bend one thumb up and down.)*

Very well, I thank you.
>   *(Bend other thumb up and down.)*

Run away,
>   *(Return one hand behind back.)*

Run away.
>   *(Return other hand behind back.)*

Repeat with each finger:
Pointer, Tall Man, Ring Man, and Pinkie